WALDEN
LANE

WALDEN
LANE

SADDLEBACK
EDUCATIONAL PUBLISHING
www.sdlback.com

ISBN-13: 978-1-68021-370-6
ISBN-10: 1-68021-370-9
eBook: 978-1-63078-585-7

Printed in Malaysia

21 20 19 18 17   1 2 3 4 5

HALLOWEEN

EVAN JACOBS

Trick or Treat

Halloween 2014

Marlon's fave costume ever: Rainbow Dash from *My Little Pony*. He was obsessed!

Best candy? For Marlon, it's Twix. For Steve, it's Skittles all the way.

Ashley knows how to sing "Let It Go" in Spanish *and* Italian.

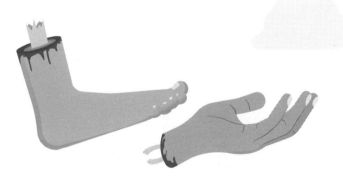

To Kayla, Halloween is all about scary: zombies, severed limbs, oozing blood. Epic!

Chapter 1
Tricked

I'm almost 14," Marlon said. "Why does Ashley have to come? I go out alone all the time."

It was Halloween.

Marlon's parents were sitting in the living room. An old horror movie was on TV. It was in black and white. A candy bowl sat by the front door.

Mr. and Mrs. Moore wore costumes. Marlon's dad was dressed as a clown. He wore a blue-and-gold bodysuit. His face was painted white. On his nose was a big red circle. Embarrassing!

His mom was dressed in a prison jumpsuit. It was orange. She had worn it to work that day. Marlon's mom was an elementary school teacher. All her students loved her costume.

"Because it's at night," his mom said. "You know you're not allowed to go out alone."

"And it's Halloween," his dad said.

Their eyes were glued to the movie. Both ate candy. Marlon felt like he was talking to two big kids. Who were these people?

Marlon was dressed as Captain America. The costume came with a plastic shield. He looked buff.

"So what?" Marlon said. "I'm going to be with Steve. We won't get in any trouble."

Steve McCain was Marlon's best friend. They always went trick-or-treating together. The boys hung out at the middle school. They were in the eighth grade. Next year they would be in high school.

Steve was going as Iron Man. Marlon had already seen his friend's costume. The costume had a cool mask.

"Don't think I'm happy either," Ashley said. She came down the stairs. "I've got a party to go to. What about *my* curfew? It's at 10. There will be no time for fun. Let's get this over with."

It was six o'clock. Ashley only had to be with the boys until eight. Marlon wanted to wait until it was darker. But he didn't want to waste time.

Ashley was dressed as Elsa from *Frozen*. She wore Elsa's sparkly dress. It came with silver slippers. Her wavy black hair was now in one big braid.

"See?" Marlon said. "Ashley's not going to be any fun. She just wants to get to her party."

"Marlon," his dad said. "You're leaving now. You'll have plenty of time."

"Yeah," Ashley said. "They're making me walk you guys for two hours."

"Two hours?" Marlon whined.

Mrs. Moore looked up from the movie. "The neighborhood's not that big, honey."

The Moores lived in a city called Walden Lane. The small city was like many others. It was made up of homes, apartments, and businesses. Walden Lane was surrounded by beautiful hills. There were places to hike. Some parts of town were nice. Other parts were rundown.

Marlon's parents were right. The neighborhood wasn't big. Still, he loved Halloween. He didn't want to feel rushed. He had a big goal. It was to get as much candy as possible.

"Do you want one of us to take you?" his dad asked, smiling.

"Yeah, little brother." Ashley was smiling too. "Have Mom or Dad take you."

"No!" Marlon screeched.

Going with Ashley was bad enough. She didn't want to go trick-or-treating. Ashley felt too old for that now.

Big sister or parents? He chose big sister. It was better than going with his parents. Marlon hadn't trick-or-treated with them in two years. He didn't want people he knew to see him. He'd be the joke of the school. No eighth graders trick-or-treated with their parents!

"Then get your shield, Captain," Ashley said. "You're wasting time."

Marlon looked at his parents. They smiled at him and shrugged. He picked up his shield. Then Marlon followed Ashley out the front door.

Chapter 2
Babysitter

So many kids were out trick-or-treating. The streets were full of costumed candy seekers. Many parents dressed up too. There were Avengers, a Batman, *Star Wars* characters, pirates, and princesses.

Marlon, Steve, and Ashley had been out for 45 minutes. It was dark and cold now. Walden Lane always felt crisp in the fall.

"We've got a lot of stuff," Steve said.

He held up his bag. "It's over halfway full."

"Yeah," Marlon said. "Maybe going earlier wasn't a mistake."

"I told you," Ashley said. "You guys are lucky to have me with you."

Ashley didn't look up from her phone. She had been texting the whole time. But she'd also stayed close to the boys.

Steve's parents normally took them trick-or-treating. But they had plans this year. Steve was going to spend the night.

"Even Steve's parents let us walk by ourselves," Marlon said. "As long as they could see us."

Across the street, Marlon spotted Jake Dyson and Tim Ochoa. They were two of the coolest kids at the school. There were no parents around them. No older siblings either.

"Look," Marlon said to Steve. "They're out by themselves."

"Yeah," Steve said.

"My parents think being out alone at night is bad," Marlon said. "But it's just like being out in the day. Somebody could jump me just as easily."

"Maybe if you acted more mature," Ashley said. She still hadn't looked up from her phone. "But you don't, Marlon. That's your problem. You used to be really scared of the dark, remember?"

"That was when I was a kid," he snapped. "I'm not scared of anything now."

"Not anything?" Ashley looked up at him.

"Nope."

Ashley eyed her brother. She smiled slightly. Then she went back to texting.

"Yeah," Steve chimed in. He didn't want to be left out. "I'm not scared of anything either."

"You're two tough guys, huh?" Ashley asked. "You're not afraid of anyone or anything."

"What's there to be afraid of?" Marlon asked. "Nothing bad has ever happened to us."

"I was camping one time," Steve said. "And a bear walked right past my tent. My parents were scared. I wasn't."

Walden Lane also had open spaces. There were many parks too. It wasn't just packed with neighborhoods and strip malls. The group walked along some open space. There were a few streetlights. They were placed far apart. The lights lined a long road.

It was very dark. It seemed like everybody had disappeared.

Marlon was excited. They would be in a new neighborhood soon. What could it mean? More candy!

The three of them walked for a while.

But no new neighborhood appeared. In fact, the road got even darker.

They now stood in front of the city's graveyard.

Chapter 3
Trick-or-Treat Deal

The graveyard was huge. It had a tall iron fence around it. The fence seemed to go on and on. It was black and blended with the night. A road led up to the graveyard gate. This was for car's to drive through.

The guys looked past the entry gate. Tombstones lined the road. The stones ran right to the gate. The boys' eyes followed the road. It led to an office. Behind that was a large shed. There was a dim light on in the office window.

As dark as it was, they could still see the graves. The light from the moon lit up the area. There were a few tall trees. The branches were long. They looked like gnarly arms.

"Let's keep going," Marlon said.

He eyed his candy again. The boys had a lot of treats. Still, Marlon wanted more. In the far distance, he saw another neighborhood.

"Yeah," Steve said.

"What's the matter?" Ashley asked. She put down her phone. "Are you scared?"

"No," they said.

"Doesn't sound like it," Ashley replied, smiling.

"You can't trick-or-treat here," Marlon said. "It's not right."

"Yeah," Steve said. "It's disrespectful."

"The light's on." Ashley pointed toward it. The office was far. "And the gate's open." She pointed to the gate.

The boys turned to look at it. Ashley was right. The gate to the graveyard hung open a few inches. It moved slightly in the wind.

The graveyard was haunted. Everyone knew it. Nobody went there unless they had to. And you never went there at night. People had seen ghosts.

Marlon and Steve had heard all the stories. They never believed them. Thankfully, they had never had a reason to visit.

"They're probably just going home now," Marlon said. "They're not giving out candy."

"Why would the lights be on? They probably want visitors." Ashley stared at her brother. The two boys thought they were so cool. "You guys aren't scared of anything, right?"

Marlon and Steve looked at each other.

"It's okay." Ashley started to walk away from the gate. "Captain America and Iron Man are scared of a graveyard. No big deal."

"We're not," Marlon said. "We just don't have much time. It's dumb to walk that far. They may not have any candy."

"I'll make you a deal." Ashley turned toward them. "You guys go in there. Walk to that office. See if you can trick-or-treat. Do that and I'll back off."

"You'll go home?" Marlon asked. He was excited.

"No," Ashley said. "I'll just give you more space."

"A lot more space?" Steve asked.

"Like you're not even here?" Marlon said.

"Like I'm not even here."

Marlon and Steve looked at each other again.

"Deal," they said.

Chapter 4
Graveyard Road

Marlon, Ashley, and Steve walked down the graveyard road. They could see the faint lights from the small office. The graveyard was dark otherwise. There were no lights along the road. The only light came from the moon.

"This place looks really old," Marlon said.

"It's been here 30 years," Ashley said.

"Really?" Steve asked. "That makes it super old."

Ashley was still on her phone. Marlon wanted her to use it as a flashlight. He wasn't going to ask her, though. Ashley would think he was scared. Then she might call off the deal. They only had a little over an hour. Then trick-or-treating would be over.

There was a cracking sound. Marlon and Steve jumped. Where had the sound come from?

The wind blew harder. Why now? It was creepy.

Marlon and Steve scanned the graveyard. They were halfway to the office. It looked like a small house. The one-story office was white. It had a tile roof. The front door was red. The office didn't look like it belonged.

"This place is kind of cool," Marlon

said. He was scared. But he told himself not to worry. They would be leaving soon.

"Cool?" Steve said. "I wouldn't use that word."

"I guess I meant in a scary way," Marlon said.

"Or a dead one?" Ashley said.

Marlon and Steve looked at her. The light from her phone glowed under her face. She looked like a monster.

"Yeah." Marlon looked at the office. "I guess I forgot about that."

"Don't worry." Ashley went back to texting. "We're almost there."

Marlon walked a little faster. Steve followed his lead.

They finally stood in front of the office. Two steps led up to the red door. The dim light appeared to flicker. Huh. Creepy!

"I wonder if it's too late to knock," Marlon said.

"You're not going to chicken out now, are you?" Ashley asked.

"I'm not chickening out," Marlon said.

"Yeah," Steve agreed. "We just don't want to be rude."

"You don't want to be rude?" Ashley said. "Ha-ha! Since when have you two cared about being rude?"

Marlon and Steve eyed each other.

"You want to go—"

"You go first," Steve said, interrupting.

Ashley laughed.

Marlon took a deep breath. He walked up to the front door. Marlon could feel his friend behind him.

Marlon stared at the red door. The red looked darker up close. Marlon had a thought. Was the door actually painted in blood? It sure looked like it.

"Knock on it!" Steve ordered.

"I will!"

Steve could be pushy sometimes. Especially when he was scared.

Marlon knocked on the door.

Nothing happened.

He knocked again. "Well, Ashley," he said. "I guess nobody's here."

"Bummer," Steve said.

The boys turned back to face Ashley.

But she was gone!

Chapter 5
Locked In

Ashley," Marlon said slowly. "Ashley?"

He couldn't believe it. A second ago she had been behind them. Now she was gone.

"Where did she go?" Steve asked.

"I don't know," Marlon said. He was nervous.

Marlon moved away from the office. Steve followed.

"Ashley! Ashley!" Marlon called.

There was no answer. It was as if his sister had vanished.

"My sister can't just disappear. That's impossible," Marlon said.

"What do you want to do?" Steve asked. He moved closer.

"I want to bail."

"Let's go!" Steve started walking back to the road.

"But we can't," Marlon said. "We can't just leave my sister."

"Maybe she left too," Steve said. "She could've been scared."

Marlon knew his sister didn't leave. What was going on? "I don't think she left," he said. "We would've heard her."

"Maybe she's like Quicksilver."

The character was from *X-Men*. He moved really fast. Nobody could keep up.

"She's not that fast, Steve."

Marlon scanned the graveyard. It

seemed even darker now. He could barely see the grave markers. The trees seemed to have disappeared in the darkness.

"So what do you want to do?" Steve was getting impatient. He was scared.

Marlon was scared too. He couldn't leave his sister, though. "Let's look around," he said.

"You want to look around. Are you crazy? Here? At night?"

"Do we have another choice?" Marlon asked.

It was 20 minutes later. Ashley hadn't reappeared. Marlon and Steve had walked around the graveyard. They knew it was bad luck to step on people's graves.

The graveyard had two rows of trees. They were on the left and right sides. The trees lined the fence. The boys had even looked around the trees. The branches reached out as if to grab them. It was unnerving.

Ashley was nowhere to be found.

They were on the left side of the graveyard. Marlon and Steve were standing by one of the big trees. Its trunk was large. There were no low branches. The tree creaked in the wind.

"I think we should call the cops," Steve said.

"Did you bring your phone?" Marlon asked.

"Nope. I had nowhere to put it." Steve held out his arms. "My costume doesn't have pockets."

"Neither does mine," Marlon said. He held up his shield. It attached to his wrist with straps. "I didn't really think about it.

I could've hacked my shield. Made some kind of pocket."

"*M-a-a-a-r-l-o-o-o-n*," a voice called in the wind.

The boys' jaws dropped.

"Did someone just call your name?" Steve asked.

"I think," Marlon said. "Maybe."

They looked around.

"*M-a-a-a-r-l-o-o-o-n*," the voice called again.

"Let's get out of here!" Marlon yelled.

"Yeah!" Steve agreed with a scream.

They took off across the graveyard. Marlon and Steve were careful not to run on any graves. Their luck was already bad.

"Almost there!" Marlon called.

They reached the gate. Oh no! Help! It was locked.

Chapter 6
Bewitched

It's locked? What do you mean?" Steve yelled.

"It's locked!" Marlon pointed to the closed padlock. "Look at it!" He was freaking out.

"What are we going to do now?" Steve whispered. His face was white.

"This is a big graveyard," Marlon said. "There's got to be another way out."

Marlon looked around in the darkness. The moon had shifted. Light was coming up from behind the tombstones. The trees cast spooky shadows. The graveyard looked even scarier.

Then Marlon noticed something. The light inside the graveyard office … It was off!

"Marlon," Steve said. "What happened to the light in the office?"

"I … I don't know," Marlon said slowly. Then he turned to the fence. "Maybe we can climb it?"

"Marlon," Steve said. He eyed the fence too. "It's way taller than us."

"We have to do something!" Marlon yelled.

"Maybe we can dig a hole. Then we'll go under it." Steve eyed the ground.

"Genius. And what are we going to dig with?" Marlon asked.

"Isn't there a shed behind the office?"

"You really want to go back over there?" Marlon asked. He put down his bag of candy. Marlon put his hands on the bars of the fence. "Give me a boost."

"You're crazy," Steve said.

Steve locked his fingers together. He crouched down slightly. Marlon put his foot onto Steve's cradled hands.

"Now!" Marlon took a deep breath. "Hoist me up."

"Okay."

Steve moved himself upward. Marlon rose a bit.

"Keep going!" Marlon called.

"I can't!" Steve said through gritted teeth.

Marlon held on to the fence. He tried to pull himself up. The top was so close. If he reached it, he could leap over. Marlon could go get help.

"You're almost there!" Steve said.

Marlon started to get tired. His arms ached. He tried lifting his foot over. It was too high. He lost his grip!

"Aahhh!" Marlon yelled. He fell to the ground. Steve did his best to break his friend's fall. It wasn't enough.

Marlon hit the ground with a thud.

"Are you okay?" Steve asked.

"Yeah," Marlon said. "I think."

"That was a good try."

"You know something?" Marlon said. "Captain America makes it look a lot easier in the movies."

"*M-a-a-a-r-l-o-o-o-n*," the voice called again. "*S-t-e-e-e-v-v-v-e*."

What the what?! The boys freaked out.

Their eyes practically popped out of their skulls.

"It said my name again!" Marlon sat up.

"It said my name too!"

"There is no escape," the creepy voice said.

The boys looked around the graveyard. They couldn't tell where the scary voice was coming from.

"*M-a-a-a-r-l-o-o-o-n*!" The voice was louder now. "*S-t-e-e-e-v-v-v-e*!"

"The voice is getting louder!" Marlon gasped.

"Does that mean it's closer?" Steve whispered.

"Yes!" the voice screeched.

The boys turned around.

There was a witch behind them! Her face was white. Red lips looked like the color of fresh blood. Her black dress swirled. On her head was a hat. It was crazy big and came to a point.

"How do you like it here?" she cried.

Marlon and Steve stared at her. They were terrified. The boys couldn't speak.

"How do you like your new home?" she asked. She raised her arms in the air.

The two took off. They tore across the graveyard. The boys ran over graves this time. Bad luck? How could it get worse? They were truly afraid.

"Aahhh," they screamed. Surely their screams would wake the dead.

They ran past the office. The light was still off. They didn't stop. Then they reached the other side of the graveyard. The iron fence stopped them. A large tree grew next to it.

"Marlon," Steve sobbed as he tried to breathe.

"I know, dude. We need to get out of here," Marlon cried.

"That was a real witch!" Steve screamed.

"I know!" Marlon said.

"She was *so* creepy." Steve's voice cracked.

They were breathing hard. Then they heard a sound. It was a rattling noise. The boys looked up. The tree above them shook violently.

Something fell to the ground.

Chapter 7
The Shed

Marlon and Steve stepped back from the tree. The object hit the ground. Hard.

A body!

It wore a white shirt. The body had green pants on. And a green suit jacket. It also wore brown shoes. Was it a man? It looked like it had been human once.

Marlon and Steve noticed something else.

Blood!

There was a lot of it. It was all over the man's shirt collar. It was right where his head should have been.

"Marlon," Steve said slowly. "He doesn't have a head."

"You're right." Marlon's voice was low. He wasn't even sure Steve had heard him.

Then the man's arm twitched.

Marlon and Steve jumped.

"He's still alive!" Steve screamed.

"Steve," Marlon hissed. "Calm down. He's obviously dead."

"Calm down? We're locked in a graveyard! There's a witch after us! A body just fell from a tree!"

"Are you okay?" Marlon asked.

"That's a stupid question!" Steve said.

The headless body suddenly sat up.

"Aahhh!" Marlon and Steve screamed.

Again, they ran through the graveyard. This time in the opposite direction.

The boys didn't look back. They were too panicked.

Marlon spotted the shed. It was behind the office. He ran over to it. Steve followed him.

It was locked.

"No!" Steve cried. "What do we do now?"

Marlon had never seen his best friend so scared. He looked back. The headless body was gone. Where did it go?

Marlon didn't say a word. Steve would realize it soon enough.

"Why didn't we bring our phones?" Steve whined.

"We just need a weapon," Marlon said.

"We need to get out of here!"

Marlon tried to pull open the shed door.

"Marlon," Steve said. His voice trembled. "I don't see the headless body. It's not on the ground."

Marlon closed his eyes. Wake up! Wake up! This was just a bad dream. He wanted a Halloween do-over.

"It isn't?" Marlon acted surprised. He knew Steve was close to losing it. "Let's go back to the fence."

"Why?"

"I think it's our best chance to escape."

"We tried and almost died."

"We didn't almost die, Steve."

Boom!

Something inside the shed slammed against the door. The shed shook. The boys quickly moved away.

"Remember that camping story I told you? About the bear?" Steve asked.

"Yeah."

Their eyes were glued to the shed.

"It was a lie. A bear never walked past me. It was a raccoon," Steve said. "See? I am not brave. What do you think is in there?"

"I don't know," Marlon said. "And I don't want to find out."

Boom!

Chapter 8
No Escape

The door flew open. The boys took off. They weren't going to wait around. Neither wanted to see what had come out of the shed.

They ran toward the front gate.

Were dogs chasing them? They could hear paws pounding. And vicious barking. The dogs sounded big, loud, and mean.

"They are going to kill us, Marlon!" Steve screamed. "Those dogs are going to rip our throats out. Then they'll eat us alive!"

"Just keep running!" Marlon shouted. "We've got to get away from them!"

The pounding and barking suddenly stopped. What had happened?

Marlon and Steve slowed up a bit.

Stomp! Stomp!

Stomping? What was next? Marlon swore he felt the ground shake.

The stomping got louder.

Marlon finally looked back. What was it? He didn't see a thing.

"Marlon," Steve called. "It's open!"

Marlon turned. He looked straight ahead. The gate was open!

They were going to get out. It would be okay! Maybe Ashley had left. Was she all right?

Marlon hoped she was on the other side. Maybe she was waiting for them.

The boys ran faster. They were 50 yards from the gate.

Then the witch sprang up from the ground. She appeared out of nowhere. Oh my God! The witch was just a few feet away. She could almost touch them.

"Going somewhere?" the witch asked, smiling.

"Aahhh!" Marlon and Steve screamed. Would this nightmare never end? Just when they had some hope, it vanished.

Marlon grabbed his friend. They turned and ran back toward the graves. It was exactly where they didn't want to be.

Stomp! Stomp!

Again? They could hear the loud stomps. The sound grew louder. But where was it coming from? The boys couldn't tell what was making the noise.

"Did something else come out of the shed?" Marlon asked. "Where are those dogs?"

"I don't know," Steve said. "Maybe something ate them."

"Something else from the shed?"

"Maybe whatever is stomping popped up from below," Steve said. "Only the dogs came from the shed."

The boys looked around.

The witch was after them again. And now the headless man was too. No!

"The tree!" Steve yelled. "We'll climb it. The branches hang over the fence. That's how we'll escape."

"Yeah!" Marlon said.

The boys ran over to the tree.

The witch was so close. The headless man was behind her. And then there was the stomping. What was it? Where was it coming from?

Marlon was frightened. He wasn't strong like Steve. Steve liked to go camping. He climbed trees with ease.

Marlon wasn't like that. He liked being outside. But nature was weird. It could be hot or cold. The rain could come down like cats and dogs. He liked video games and the Internet more. The sofa was *way* better than a steep trail.

Marlon told himself to focus. They had to escape! The two had to climb the tree.

Chapter 9
Crack!

Marlon and Steve were in the tree. Steve had gone up first. He was standing on a long branch. It was thick. The branch looked sturdy. It extended over the graveyard fence.

Marlon was still climbing. He didn't climb trees much. And he was afraid of heights.

"Just pull yourself up!" Steve yelled.

"Help me!" Marlon called.

Steve had easily climbed the tree. He loved climbing. There were natural grooves on the tree's trunk. He used those to anchor his feet.

Marlon was doing the same thing. He just wasn't doing it well.

"I can't!" Steve said.

"Why not?" Marlon asked.

"Because you'll pull me down."

Marlon looked out over the graveyard. His worst fears were coming true.

The witch and the headless man were only a few yards away. The stomping sound continued. What the heck was it? The boys couldn't tell where it was coming from.

As Marlon moved up, he dropped his bag of candy. It fell to the ground.

"Darn it!" he said.

"You can have mine," Steve called. "Just keep moving!"

Steve started to move across the thick

branch. Smaller branches stuck up around him. A few even reached over the fence. Steve used them to keep his balance.

Marlon moved as fast as he could. But he was having trouble. His footing didn't feel right. The grooves felt weird on his feet. Maybe it was his shoes. It took him longer to climb.

Marlon eventually stood on the thick branch too.

Steve was halfway across. Marlon moved slowly behind his friend.

"Going somewhere?" a voice asked.

The boys looked down.

It was the witch! She stood on the ground. Her hands were on the tree's trunk.

Marlon was terrified. "Do you think she can bring this tree down?" he asked. "Can her magic make us fall?"

"Keep moving!" Steve said.

Marlon went faster.

Steve had almost reached the top of the fence. He moved carefully.

"*M-a-a-a-r-l-o-o-o-n*!" the witch called.

The headless man walked up. He stood behind her. "*S-t-e-e-e-v-v-v-e*!" he cried.

Marlon and Steve had no choice. If they didn't get across, they were dead!

Crack!

They looked at each other. A cold feeling spread through Marlon's body. The branch had to hold them! It was their only way out.

Was it breaking?

The boys had no choice. They had to keep going. Steve moved carefully. Marlon followed. They tried to keep their balance.

Crack!

The thick branch swayed. It was breaking! How long would it hold?

"Almost there!" Steve called.

"You hear that?" Marlon yelled at the witch. "We're almost out."

Snap! Crack!

The boys screamed as they fell to the ground.

Thud!

They landed.

To Marlon's surprise, he felt okay. Nothing was broken.

They had landed a few feet apart. Steve sat up. He rubbed his head.

"Ugh," Marlon said.

"No," Steve moaned.

They were still inside the graveyard.

The fierce spooks waited nearby. The stomping sound was horribly close.

Chapter 10
The Reveal

Marlon and Steve slowly stood up. The witch smiled. It was a big smile. Her eyes were wide open. Behind her was the headless man. He moved toward them. His arms were thrust forward. The man looked like a zombie.

"Leave us alone!" Marlon yelled. He pulled off his fake shield. Marlon threw it at the headless man. It hit him on his bloody collar.

"Owww!" the headless man cried.

The witch quickly turned. She looked at him. "Are you okay?" she asked.

What? This was weird! How could a plastic toy hurt a freakish monster?

"No!" the headless man cried. "He hit me right in the face."

"But you don't have a face," Marlon said.

Why were they acting like this? Marlon didn't get it. It was as if the spooks were alive. Like real people.

"Are you scared?" the witch asked. She glared at the boys. "You should be!"

"Leave us alone!" Steve cried. "We didn't do anything."

Stomp! Stomp! Stomp!

What was that? It was so loud now.

The boys backed up. There was nowhere to go. The witch and headless man moved forward. They could reach out and touch them.

"Are you scared?" the spooky freaks asked.

"Yes!" Marlon screamed. "Yes! We're scared! Okay? We're scared. Please let us go. Please."

Smack!

The boys backed into something solid. They jumped! Then Marlon and Steve turned around.

Ashley!

She was holding a portable speaker. Her phone was attached. The stomping noise came from the speaker.

The witch took off her hat. Marlon and Steve saw that it was Kayla. She was in theater at Walden Lane High School. The boys knew she was a good actress. Kayla was also Ashley's best friend.

The headless man pulled off his costume. A boy Marlon and Steve didn't know was underneath.

"You guys are Ashley's friends," Marlon said. He was still shaken up. So was Steve.

"And you guys aren't scared of anything," Ashley said, smiling. "Right?"

"Wrong!" Steve said.

"Punked!" Ashley said. She was tired of their complaining. So she had set up this plan. She had been texting her friends the entire time. Oh snap!

First she'd texted Kayla. Kayla was going to be a witch for Halloween.

Then she texted Dave Williams. Dave was the sound expert in Kayla's drama class. He loved sound effects. Dave also loved making gory costumes. The headless man costume was made of latex.

Fun fact. Dave's grandparents managed the graveyard.

Ashley had put it all together. It had been planned since the summer. She'd wanted to teach the boys a lesson. Her friends had set up the scene. They had been to the graveyard earlier in the day. Dave had created sound effects.

Everyone had a good laugh. Steve and Marlon were still a little shaken. But they had to admit, it was the best punk ever.

Ashley walked the boys home. She'd meet up later with her friends.

"No matter how old you are," she said. "You can still be scared. People need to look out for you."

It was a little after eight o'clock. Ashley was done with her trick-or-treat duties. She could go to her party soon.

They were almost back home.

"Well, you got us. I was really scared." Marlon had retrieved his candy. He held up his bag. "I'm so glad I got this back!"

The boys had so much candy.

"I'm sorry if we were jerks," Marlon said. "I was lame."

"Yeah," Steve added.

"It's okay, guys," Ashley said. "I'm used to it."

"Thanks for taking us tonight," Marlon said. "I love Halloween."

"Yeah," Steve agreed.

"This is one Halloween we'll never forget," Marlon said.

"There's always next year." Ashley laughed.

"Nah," Marlon said. "I'll be too old. This is probably my last one."

"Me too," Steve said

The boys would be 15. Did high school freshmen still dress up?

"Really?" Ashley asked. Her tone was skeptical.

Marlon and Steve looked at each other.

"Ha-ha," Marlon said with a smirk. "Probably not."

Everyone cracked up.

More fun was coming. Halloween wasn't over. It was Friday night. Ashley had a party to go to. The boys had scary movies to watch. And there was candy! So much candy. Tonight would be epic!